A HOLYTHROAT SYMPOSIUM

Aaron Williamson

CREATION PRESS

“A HOLYTHROAT SYMPOSIUM”
by
Aaron Williamson

ISBN 1 871592 17 8

ACKNOWLEDGEMENTS:
Thanks are due to the following towards the completion of this book:

Geoffrey Hemstedt
Tertia Longmire
James Williamson

At The Heart Of the Book Are Its Voices is based on an interview between Aaron Williamson and Polly Marshall April 1992

Parts of this work have appeared in the following anthologies:

Angel Exhaust
Apples and Snakes
Red Stains
Rapid Eye

First published in 1993
by
Creation Press
83, Clerkenwell Rd. London EC1M 5RJ
Tel/Fax 071 430 9878

A HOLYTHROAT SYMPOSIUM

Within The Grain

A book is in the act of becoming. It arises from the futility of searching for its own components. Everything here is fastened into the precision of its rigid embrace; especially the futility of its search. There is to be an embarkation. All is known, charted and gridworked beforehand into the clawings of its leaves. And these spill into the merest breath of an arbitration; of decisions and of the teeth of our compulsion. Open wide. This is in the act of its becoming.

The impact of enactment is an hieroglyph indented around the word, outlining the matrix scar, a primal laceration. Above its swollen fabric a nib is tracing stitch motifs, amassing shapes and binding, retaining them by heart. Here, filigrees are spun away and textured with the imminence of unattained terrain, the contours cordened round and undulating blood. Beyond, a mirage beckoning to scaffold in its vapours. Within, the cuneiforms to suturate its stench.

Beyond the book, yet at no distance, is its aerial. Without shape or dimension, it is the very rudiment of anatomy. Or rather, it is a lightning-rod trawling for ignition. As flesh. As flesh made word made flesh. Quickly, it is discerned that the raw matter, the object of the book, is its arrival at some future date in fire. Thus, the text, snaking, arches along such devious twistings and self-delusions towards an incendiary gratification. Towards, in fact, these flames.

These crude flames which cavil at our limbs.

The motile impulses, specifically those for speech are diminished. In place, these lines of vanishment, centripetal, that conflagrate as they swallow.

In the mean time the spine begins to form, congealing through its lacings of horn and nerve. A casing is thrown out, shot through with curved bolts. These ribs, curling within the pulp, are grooved through with the static of verbiage. They hold, out front as satellite to the spine, a surface of split ridges that gape and converge in the wind. The fore-edge; our sternum. Open and then closed, dithering.

Finally, it slams and unity proffers a spatula seamed through with the texture of knots. It slides, between skin and our chest, the air and these pages, pulling with its splinters into the grain.

If the book consorts with its end at each point of inception, it is for these pages and their haste to embrace it. Swollen with the blackness of its shadowing ink, in the beat of its convulsive parturitions.

The Spatial Realm

1.

The spatial realm of the silence is a parchment skin rolled thinly into a weapon. From the threatened unrolling of its disfigured surface comes obeisance. Incisions and curses. Deplorable, unspeakable tempers bark loose from its veneer into the chasmic hush. An echo-sounder would verify an upright tunnel but the sullen menace of quiescence must not be probed. Within, a figure has chosen to occupy an unexceptional area. It moves infrequently, each time to cast a face at some imagined or unverified companion. Obscure in meaning and intention, these attitudes of visage are thrown, held briefly, and collapsed at metronomic intervals. Gradually, this catalogue of humours, at first wildly capricious, begins to seem connected. A residue of feedback is framing up the mind. The tempo is driven forward. Mugging frantically with grimaces and frowns, the movements begin to diminish: spasms to twitches, small flickerings around the eyes. Concurrent with this abatement in volume, the transformations are accelerated and the face appears to move towards its optimum portrayal. This will be an enigma. The final swift and minute adjustments are heartbreaking: so much so that we no longer wish to observe. There is something untouchable and yes, preposterous here. Petrifying. Indeed, we are captive, stricken in its stare. Our fear preserves and confirms its secret and isolation creeps in from the loss of antennae; from the loss, that is, of our response. Out of the deadlock, the distance sense is spun amok. We are going it alone. No means by which to monitor this thought and feeling. Within the silence, head to head, the ear is our mirror.

2.

The book is composed of speculative observations, each to its independent page. At the foot of the page, having considered a proposition, the reader is invited to agree or disagree. A decision proposes, numerically, another page to which the reader now turns with a view to contemplating a further speculation. Sometimes there appears to be a design to such progress, other times not. An indeterminate number of decisions, if made in series, would lead the reader out of the book; in effect would allow it to be completed. There is no indication as to whether this series will consist in a preponderance of either agreements or disagreements to construct the route. In short, there is nothing to be gained through avoiding answering each proposition with the truth of one's inclination towards it. No call, that is, for calculation or preemption.

It is striking that, being returned to some of the propositions through the ensuing itinery of pages, one's decisions, through repetition, begin to accrue a sense of conviction. It is credible that if such assurance could be converted into accustomed precepts and practised outside of the book, they would lead to an attachment which, owing to its increasing vehemency, could be taken to indicate a plausible essence to our fabric. From there, one is positioned from out of a climate of veracity towards the eternal rebus.

The profound scope and ambition of the book then, would seem to suggest a prodigious work. One capable of building a vast maze of returns and referral sufficient to afford a life-time's perusal. Oddly, this is not so. A slight volume, it has, nonetheless, pages enough to afford an extraordinary number of permutations, each of which conducts a distinct, unprecedented route. Ordinarily however, and on average, if the book is attempted it is achieved within the term of an hour.

Etymology of Screams

The text is born of yearning. It accumulates the need. Pain is stacked through its racks, stratified. The hidden veins are old wounds, wounds that won't wash, won't even show themselves, so tremulous and vulnerable. Cuts to the hand, invisible, yet still there. Unwashed. The clag of guilt for feeling the pain. The text collects it, consists in it. Sometimes the pain is glimpsed, re-limbed, only for the soul to retreat, slammed shut.

The hurt derives. The hunger, wanting to be held. Shut off the need to shut down the pain. To alleviate: the writing about something. Previous to the hurting, that something itself, written. The struggle to read it back again, to unearth the corpus. Unearthly treasure, writ large. Attempting to exhume but merely imitating the sense of loss. I need. The need itself. Autonecessity. The hurt if unmet. Shut down the pain from the hurt and then rip, tear me out.

Symbolic gratifications. Each time, the hopelessness of never being loved. As good as gold and valueless. Someone, anything else, I become. Feeling the way through urination. The shallowness of breath. A face exhibiting to the window. Entering the state of alert, this will always be so: I am detested. To shut down. The balance lost. I was shattered, realising I could be killed. Scattering the target – me – before they got me.

This I know: a system of many-selves. One for who I am and others for those who are not. I am fading. The details of life are clenched to me. Frustrations. The spite I live, I live in spite. I don't like me as I am liked, I don't like them, they don't like me as I am. The end.

But always awaking again, locked away with the pain. Entombed. Years to exhumate the fear. I stank of fear, my liver spitting it out. The stink enticed corollories, I cultivated hurt. There was a way in to the hurt and a way out. Trying to get in or out, to reify the struggle. It killed me, is killing me. I killed me before anything could reach me first. Submerged my face until no breath. The pain is what kills but without it also is death. Me, murderer of mine: guilty. I did it.

Always, the tension of being unloved and shot through with more tension. Reinforced, the cables of hurt, of pain running from arm to arm. Wiring of muscle pumped through with hatred, the project: containment. A sweetness of life brewed up and circulating in bile. Raw leathered stains blotching the stomach. I start climbing. To pull out, to retract the distress. The drag sears, rising from craw to my mouth. Speaking in urine. A dreadful fear. The worst fear conceivable. I have conceived it. Mine.

I know why the hurt is. The hate is: believe my humiliation. I am hated and believe it. As good as gold murdering yourself. Stimulation, feeding, being held, caressed; I am none of these. All of us, we look at me. Staring me down. Transformed into base metals, a heart alchemy, fired in anguish. Raging. And then: solid. Tap me and I resound. Tin surface. And on the inside, torn metal embedding the concave. The drag of hurt, each day through to night.

The affliction. Don't mention it. Untalked around. It speaks itself. Eloquent in quiescence, a sore ratifying the deadness, irreal. Yet true: actual, taking place. The inexperience of hurt, unknowing it. Burying the life-recall and then closing down. In the gullet. The fear of feeling the need in needing to feel. Afraid of the ground: the pain is grounded. A fear of the real because of the pain. The pain is real. Instead, I locate to this unease. Submerging together, killing itself in the pain. If one is rekindling the other, damp it with stale. Forget it. Forget all of it.

What is left of me from turning away from distress. Discharged into circumpsect limbs, encircling the death of me. A septic vat swilling the central node, repellance at the exoskeleton. Pull to. Pull-to the ache, bitterness and cramp. The nub-ends of nerve. Swollen inside. Pumping the shoulders with burdens, the worthlessness. Carnage. A pulsebeat between fears.

Mors ontologica. A death of the spirit. A glance, a word, a single threatening gesture. Pneumatically regulating and compressing the air into this death. Enough to pulverise the breath of life. Dust and relics attesting to dormition. Respiration is imperceptible, equalised as the exact volume of the vault is always maintained.

Screaming without reason and crying. Inside, trying to intern, to conceal the grappling of an agonised macrocosm. Pummeling and rattling, I stood there controlled and inert. For each of us. The aggregate berserking away at viscous enclosures, my hide erupting with punches. The tympanist within accentuates dementia and tears drift in from the coldest afar. Of course the sounds of the words, trapped in the torso continue with speaking. Silently. The weight and mass of them built in, impacted. Each one particular in rates of vibration. Scratching, hatching away at an escape. I am penetrated, infiltrated. Possessed by sounds which cavitate their host. They have me. I feel them. Embryos quickening with seeds of fire. Settled amongst the dust and then, crack, hurtling forth. I catch them before they reach out: no signal, no trace of an event, just me. Ingrowing. Sullen, staring, clutching on.

The upshot: I am sinking into my abdomen. Retracting to close in, to catch at their inception the distressing words. A flash pulse, grabbed at and stifled. My stomach a cresset and then: pissed out. Ashes tasting of ashes in my mouth. Mumbling the melt-down. Cinders stewing the forkfuls of phonemes.

I prostrate. The sickness itself, a language. It rises, a dankness around tidings. Controlled patternings of verbal compulsions. They fit fast together, consistent within hair-fractured glimpses through the larynx of the outer beyond. A phrasing of stubborn detachment – enticed yet resistant – shielding untold solipsists. In thralldom to its oddities, I speak and the pudenda recoils, retrenching the gizzard. Distraught. Unhinged by argot and spewing entrails. This I embody: a denizen grammar. Outcome conjectured: mors ontologica. With dung at the centre, voided.

It loses me, eludes me. A distorted contour withered and vapid, hiding, confining the I.D. It's hopeless. I take stock: this stink. Malice, therefore, always before thought. And then after, dismissal, brush the cack off. Rejectamenta.

Is this reading me out? Who lets the loss? Crossing it, stamping it off and then the disgorging. Obscene dross gagging, loathing up the gell of me. An upsurge of skin, rippling with fume, blistered around the apex. Foiled again. Baked with this chafing, seethe-crazed and blackened. An acidic mouthful nestling the cheeks, lapping the clamped molars. Impacted jawbones. I avoid all conjunctions. Discount me, an acquaintance. I'm not tolerable. I swallow it.

And yet castigating the loss of autonomy. Caught out, a fingered trap. I can't stop it. Me. I the exclusive pronounced. Defining. Outlining. Foul, filth, soil, dreck, gums, gross. You wouldn't recognise me. It never happened. How many chances, lost through inaction? Vexed? Shot through the spit in the masticators, crudding a vitality. And spinning a taste of crassness, a matter of apprehension. This is like distance. Crawling ablaze upon water. Forget it, I'm not O.K. I use you for abuse. Abrasion. In the midst of occlusion, on the inside it is shameful. My conviction. You are reading me my thoughts. Don't pause! I'm guilty. I am. Condemned.

And eager to re-inforce it, this detention. The victim is offensive. I take it, it's there. I could be asked and in replying, face off – an act of contrition. A disguise merely. Despising in the gridlock of vision, I talk through a grim tint of fixture. Unlettered. And not even ticking.

It will be interminable. A dream beyond all beckoning. The one in this pain. I swallow me, gag on the egress to push down the substance. A stiflement, gorge balking; a sin of immersion. You have to suffer. And then quaff it. Engulf the whole backdrop and pull, pull down hard. A mutual ingestion. And when the movement is finished, a small flick of the charred, distended tongue will serve to declare.

I return there. Taken back, the force pulls its gravity, a rain of sequences brimming with opulence. Reversing into fortune. I am unfortunate, disproportionally forced down against my will, held up against the image of an aberration. I can't help it. It's not right. It's wrong but it always feels right.

The victim and his fantasy, sleeping in old spaces and murdering his cringes. The attack is forefrontal, behind is a melifluent agreement, but the attack is out front. It takes off my face. And with it, a last chance of redemption. 'Hold it, that's not right, I never meant that.' It's this: I ache above board. Radiant, burning. And when the kiss to my blisters unsalivates the balm, then, I will be lost to ruin. I live and revile.

A contemptible thing inside me, living alongside me, a wink to one side, deathly but urgent. I want to let go here. To leak with the wetness of life. Not death, death is just dry. I pushed. And then pushed back. I could kill before writing of death. I have to let it. To let: a request, proposal or command. Ask me what hurts and then watch me dissolve inside splinters. Sucked back in exactly where I want to escape.

I can't, can not. Where hope persists it is futile: you want to hope and then fake it, surge on. No need for anything more than the need itself. It's in here, a page bespeaking another page and then... pages of it, trembling with forlorn derision. A happy ending. It all meets again, joined up within me. Not eating me, I'm ate. A thread of scars feasting. At the central cornu and from there, bite into the fluid and chew. Masticate this breath. Walk out of here with this offal rubbed into me, yearning for birth in its dreaming text. Eating my words, returning, not singly, but more often, collected.

A Disembodied Text

The disembodied text is another book. It is set, say, in Africa. Attempting to maximise its public potential on a global scale it is anticipating its reception into a cultural milieu. The writing presumes to situate its meaning, business-like, at the site of our capacity for compliancy in assigning objects, concepts, persons, to its words. We are set down, in Africa, surrounded by perpetual warfare; the lingua-franca of overhead weapons fire. Characters exchange dialogue, going here, moving there, assembling from within our fascination. Now, the sky is peppered with stars and the desertscape becalmed by twilight:

"Fear tinged... the knife hitting the door again... shot in the right foot... a single mercy round..."

Shot. The word operates an immediate routine vehicle to the assumed, arbitrated action. The right foot, out there in Africa, telling of its complaint. This compliancy, combined with a contriving self-consistency, will stabilise reception of the book into the machinations surrounding and described by it. We, too, are shot down by the text; our thoughts so many lame birds struggling to attain the shot.

Conversion is effortless: we grope for the design. The book leaves its confected Africa by way of airport bookstalls, its voices holding the clarity of mirage, of overheard bartering, cajoling, barely fluttering our lips as we peel the pages. Ideation becomes massively disseminated – into cultural reverbations and fiscal activity, further voices and presences, scheming behind the arras of its leaves. We only trace the surface drift of a volatile breath through random and erratic dislocations.

Along these lines, the book is an explosion, an inadvertant sandstorm. A detonation away from its own mass.

The accustomed event in which the realisation of such a book takes place, eventually is described here as the disembodiment of texts.

II

By which may be taken to imply a suspension of the body's mass when generating the text. Staging as it were, a decapitation of the mind in order for it to adhere elsewhere: in some proposed expanse, among plots and characters, escapades. Thus the disembodied text becomes the able-bodied text: a self-endowed untroublement with the borders of physique. A well-being within the acts of reading and of writing. Assumption of passage. We concede: that this was done and said, accessed, thought. A suspension of our disbelief is hurtling to its end.

And so, a shape establishes itself before its demarcation, granted out of an assumed ability to build within its gist. Unanimously. Always, the invisible centre of the disembodied text. Within, identity is fixed. We become for the interim, a specific designated float within the writer's, the publisher's drift.

The able-disembodied text mounts an appeal, deflecting observation of its unsightly metastasis *as* text. An instance: its custom to complete the page with print is its disguise, its camouflage of hygiene. Intact. Robust. Insistence upon completion and enclosure presses in, principally and signally at the cellular, profound lacuna between the diction and reception of its sense.

Invitation to transpire the book is more pressing as one approaches centrifugal forces. The proposed window upon the world is at this height – here is its view, sex, status. It sounds like this.

III

We return to Africa or any other site of imposition. This time, it is a colony of the book. An anaemic place, it is unbitten by embodiment. No remnant can be lifted into language – there is an arid beat that bears no weight, is unconcerned with mattering. The tears and blood of the place, the book with which to stain them – lost within imponderable meanderings of an absence. And this is the absence of ourselves, the readers as we defect into the writing.

A spurious escape from the ineluctible integrity of the body with its mind is hatched. Anatomy is withdrawn, the body is numbed, the mind aflight. The book accomodates, commodifies an instrument to the dulling of our pain. It skirts the blunt malaise of all its limitless entrapment. 'But yet the body is our booke'. But yet, it leads us out, forgetful of our divine trap. Into the ersatz text cavorting our ubiquitous and fretful blight.

Cacophonies

Text is integument

systematically exploited

for orbital distances

associated with

alternating

inner pulses

& verbal breaks

smear plated

across the macroscopic rhythms

of the planets

scars

ice ages

a rage of time-scales

day in and day out

rubato

at the interplay

of captivity

a tub-thump

through amytal injected

subfunctions

of handedness

& ligatured to church bells
or rainfall on the clapper
at least
syncopated
in beat to beat fluctions
staccato
tense ratio
of ricochet insertions
the arctic trigger
within mountains
and populations
each punctual by turns
and igniting a compass:

the text is tympani
the text is the mallet

Splenetic homuncule
is stretched
around the glistening
sting
of cortex instincts
neuroimaging the fabric
spirit down
around
contaminating dots of fero-shards
peeled and spread
about the hemispheres
of bursted space
& issued from the eight-sleigh
bells
which chatter the tightened clutch
of spreadracks
visible with blueing
the surface cinders
smelting
onto a pith of sinews
deep within

the fists of numen
spumed
and paring the firmaments
in nimbus sheets
that boil
out here as being
a katabatic breathing space
on stilts
the respiration
of deities
splintered among the hills
enamelling
a textured twist
with megalithic rondolets
and squeezed behind
a tightened shift
a hub of lungs
between the meal of bone:
'homuncule splenetic'

Glossolalia klaxon
a follicle cactus
extracting from scratches
the citrate dirt
veiling
and shunt-biting
through tattooed-tip cuticles
of pulverised front grinders
exhaling refractions
light-resonant
past colon-cog seizures
& dovetailed with
cross-cellular gnashing
at shadowless
yet sustenant flat idols
stab-thundered
through plasmatic damagers
some reverb-cack dendraxons
of amethyst
incision
farfalla

rough haulage scaling drag
wedge-pounding subactions
of apparatus pincers
the main-tail idalia
hybridising
of ice-claws
and horses
O ye who make haste
to pass through
hell so slowly...
bewailing transactions
and scorching the helium
of lexical aliens
inhaling the breath
of these words
it is fading
too long for this whorl

A holythroat symposium

tuned in to its neckbox

relays the static

the overlap of phonemes

pneumatic

in the pull of surges

wireless

and jabbering

the fricatives

...enough force to counteract

the suction

the turbulence

battering

time and again after

time through the

squall bursts

a palatal noise

heaped up in different

manners

the exchange of sensation

incessant

distinct
distributions of energy
a gut talk,
head to head gut talking
as regards
labiodental, linguadental...
– guttereal –
intensity referred
back into ad-hocery
those frequencies
of spectra
diminishing to flickers
pervasive voice-sources
duration   intensity   frequency
sustained into incoming
bulletins
cable-crazed, diatribes
through spirilla
and studding a facula
sheen-tendoned
ligaments and straps
the rig-up framing
lariat transmissions
emitting

diaphonous lassoes

rife-rebus in many tongues

pitch, loudness

and craw-emphasis

a pulsar turned up into surcharge

the quasi-buzz nexus

to excite the interruptives,

the noncontinuents...

THAT IS: the asterisk

pump-valved afloat

in the bitumen axis

of flat and thin signals

spew-nova

table-talk   &   blocktackle

as well: the hook-up

mongered with link-people

the vinculum of used imagery

outside of the acquired language,

primitivised by feral sickness

and engaged in halucinoids

and STRATIFYING

RAMIFYING

a spargefacting diaspora

through intersecting meshwork:

uniformity   indicated
in the points   eloquently by
of view   brain
altered   preverbal
dichotomous   in organism
rapid spectral   representing
changes   intensity
in time   as one
picked up   dimension
between   coiling
relays before
compacted
all about it
become   being
centred a   clustered
vox sustain   stimuli
into its nasals   harmonic
& antiformants   periodics
glides and   concentrating
semivowels   the feedback
yammering   of beyond
impedance   along channel
spray and   and cavity
emerging   & merging

INTERROBANG THE <u>BRAKE</u>

citation:

(breathe here)

but for the sake of

densification

and since the passional ambidextres

are unknown...

ADPRESS THE SYZYGY

its synechdoche

– dystrophy –

& pushing up tresses

upon tresses

curlycueing with diphthongs

rasping

at the seraphim intake

(breathe here again)

AN OVERHANG OF SPAKE

cascading hirsute

commencement

significant in measure

meant:

HARANGUE ITS ACHE

chimeric crank underhand

echoic refund

of REMANENT

a FAKE

reMAKE

...swilled under this jaw-clamp

I-said-swilling

(the sheer phonetic drive

of an ever-deepening

pocket of sense:

posterity, particularly,

is always trying to catch up...)

on the GIBSTAFF

angle-cantilevered signalflake

in the CAN CAN of a CORNCRAKE

...in the sounding of a bradawl

placed gently in contact with a denture's glint

– waiting –

(until)

you SAID IT

sssssssssssssssssssss

At The Heart Of The Book Are Its Voices

"At the heart of the book are its voices..."

"A rich stream of things going off all the time" he said, "an involuntary witness to statements, phrases, knocks and bangs; things like this all day long. So consequently..."

"Protecting yourself from the barrage of contempt, sorry, temporaries: contemporary life and how this..."

"Yes, I would agree. A personal initiative around language. I think the initiative to think and say original things is greatly undermined. Currently."

(Silence. A gap proceeding into:)

(Unintelligible) "...yes, I think conflict has a peculiar flavour to it and sometimes a subliminal nature to it as well, where for example with complementary colours and statements..."

"Is that what you're expressing with 'open and then closed'...?"

"'In the same breath together'... Yes, that's pretty much about that. Conjoining things."

"Making a circle?"

"Yes, that's right. Although an uncompleted circle."

(No rejoinder. Protracted calm. Sighs, cups lifted and replaced.)

*

"...an architectural metaphor to describe how the anatomy becomes rigid..."

"And how we build ourselves?"

"Yes. Particularly if the vacillation of language – of giving and receiving through its apparatus – is severed and adrift, confused. So it's a way of re-aligning one's experience and projection of language back to its unified source..."

"Trying to observe the soundable..."

"Trying to activate a type of physical awareness that, by its own form of nature is deposited in and constrained by the body. Thus, this host, its dross, is unbridled; re-activated at the source of the trauma, become a part, perhaps even the dominant communication of a piece of text."

"And this is just a piece of text?"

"Yes. It is, as they say, just a part of itself. The desire is that it could begin to be something else."

*

“...no, what it is is that I’m seeking to develop conditions for the book to take place in.”

“Well... this isn’t simply the maturance of a particular talent?”

“That’s right. This is how the book is acquired... a sort of nascent mechanism which seeks out and explores its own make up. So it’s there all the time and...”

“Yes. I like that. I’m opposed to there being any particular mode... you know, writing, thinking, reading. It’s a passive state, so a lot of modern conventions about messages... slogans for example... are working their way in. In speaking of writing a deafness, the implication is also towards a type of immunity.”

*

(Later.)

“So, conceivably, the book could take place before it was actually able to say these things...?”

“Perhaps. Who could say? Perhaps not.”

A Thread of Scars

The sensual knot
rooted in annihilation
arriving through earth
its stillness
slipping
past lucent benchmarks
in a sky of lines
the star on its leash
pulling in the quiet deaths
of sentient cruel waters

An artery awash
impart of tide lines
evince map-rings
pith-strung and held
inside quartz
wheeling down nerves
lifts
a bracelet of mists
grazing the panic bolt's
arterial latrine of push petals

Astral connivent
sub-binding horizon light
swollen husks
pigging the glint
of an uncharted   glance
to the robing of feet
metallic in pulse only
for there, in the snag of yarn:
astrocytic intwining

With blood at a teething ring
lulling of silk
phantoming friction
along luminous eczma
spangled
to the cicatrix
ambiting fate before pulling in
one more
flexing of mottled psalm
– blood: at the axis

A spindle of warm cable
          glows
        as it drips
    to an ice needle
circling with splendour
and carving a membrane
with wound-movements
a lace of looped eyelids, propounding

Veracity's a drawstring
dab-dashed afleck with shadowing
flare light betingling
a solid dark
fettering of old radiances
hefting
concommitant energies, filaments
through planetary bake of salt
and its baubles
pausing to tauten with knots

Solo Boy

A four year old boy
resides in a small room
within a remote building
filled with starched adults
he remembers his parents
and begins to feel
their absence palpably
as part of the room
and why he is in it
the adults have words
for him and a use
Tabula Rasa they call him
clean slated
is the Solo Boy
'he isn't even here'

languageless
magnetised
and driven into here
as the embodiment
of its polarity
this place of conversation
of massive convolutions
dialect, diction, discourse

...constituted in and through language rather than providing its ultimate source

the boy is padded round
walls soaked through
with sterile terminology
This basement place
of Babel
–it isn't hard to see
in them what they see
in him
after all, they define it

...without co-namer
discoverer
co-sustainer

...virtually no human
reality
the animal world

an environment of gaps

It is a strange love
they have conceived
for him here
one would
sooner call it
(as he cannot)
a passion

he dwells within
and gazes through
a state of Eden
not a wonder, then,
that they want
the Solo Boy in here
to be discredited
with words
they too have a language
gap
precisely of the size
and outline of
the Solo Boy

...unable to tell lies
or be ashamed

linguistically designates:
there is no other world

they are looking for
yet cannot see
or find
themselves

At night the Solo Boy dreams of his parents' love. In this, he is stretched between them as an arch connecting them, their eyes down to their navels. He is the span of their streaming animism. They move against him slowly, spitting gently into his mouth and ears, filling him with feral sicknesses and tastes of all the life to come. Stretched around each other now, they bite and swallow bits of body parts: fingers, a toe, the Boy's breast, the mother's shoulder, the father's hair. The family has no lexical remains. It is a figure, a heart without a name. The hybrid moves, crablike around the bed, the walls, eating itself together. What is left of the Solo Boy is happy here. And yet, fermenting in his bile, the drastic onslaught of the spheres: he is rested. The itch returns, eyes breaking onto the morning walls. Today the same entanglement: walls, polish, a parent-shape that waves and mugs at him for hours. Inevitably, he bites. The Solo Boy is biting off his words in ecstasies of heat. Restrained, he is tied down, uncoupled from the space in which he moves. The lesson is one of essentials: he has yet to name something. Not so much for its own properties, but for the fact that it is not a part of him.

The first task: (pointing), 'Not me, not me and that's NOT ME'. But of course, the Solo Boy is biting off the air instead...

perceives:
not so much the people
around him, but the
invisible frisson
and tensions caused
by their perplexions
within an endless maze
of routings and referrals
filing cabinets fill up
equipment arrives
casebooks, articles,
word upon words
trying to get through
to the Solo Boy
...snap him out?
To spring him?
In any case he sits there
usually
in a corner
neither here nor there
yet boggled
with his amorphosis
his wordless extension
into pioneering
technologies
and then he starts
to remember
or perhaps not
it is so strange with
all the lighting
is he trying to resist
his anamnesis
or does he raise his eyes
to lock with the
proportion, its symbolic?
without refined divisions

soon, words will be
needed to experience
even this isolation –
something else was
introduced
the host agenda
to the miraculous
functions and
enchantments of words:
the Law
and the Law is identified
with the silent, distant
relative, the father
he whose silence speaks
of the overload
dormant with

the commentators say
without these categories
interpretations of reality
are limited because
reality must be
dismantled
divided and differentited
no reason, don't ask
so he doesn't
his parents though
at four years old
the distance between his
current isolation
and the days when he
was warm and felt
desired is already
one half of his life
& this is how he feels
his age
older than anyone
around him
aged and blended
into a primordial silence
that has long been lost
and which his palpable
frame encases
they want it, he has it
or rather, they want
to dissolve it
into the air should it be
infectious
but of course this can be
achieved only through
interrupting and
ending it
all day banging away

the explosiveness
of tongues
protector
containing
bursting with the
stiflement
of words
but before this
prior to
the horrific
overwhelming shock
of initiation

is the world surrounding
& embodied
by the Solo Boy

at the familiar narratives
of the happy tales
of release: C-A-T
say 'cat'
CATTTT
the Solo Boy agrees:
yes, there it is.
The cat too: I am happy.
Only the shaping
of the scrawled and
sounded characters
have something mournful
in their tone
sad and left out:
he hasn't got it.
'Separation from society
...inflicts unbearable
psychological tensions
upon the individual...'
but the Solo Boy
wouldn't know this
until later
at some point where he
could learn how
to enunciate such ideas.

'the limits of language
are the limits of our
world'

No. The limits of
language are the limits
of language.
For here is the
person before language.
Not able, finally,
to disappear. Capable
of human form.

Being something
without also
saying it
(psychologically tense)
surely a slip
of contra-diction
from his vigilant
enthusiasts?

This time the boy's dream is lucid, more complex. He dreams of his parents standing on either side of tall, metal doors. One parent distinguishes itself as the father and begins fixing paper guillotines of various sizes to the doors, bolting them on. He's testing and ensuring the swiftness of the handles' lunge. Oiling. The Solo Boy looks down at the protruberance from his chest. It is flexing with charges until, at the point of petrifaction, it relaxes out into a funnel, bubbling with liquids within. He looks to the mother-parent. And back into the funnel. The possibility of trajectoring between the two has been cancelled by the lack of muscular constraint.

Catalepsy

1

Emerged and lifted
into a dark cage built
with bitten steel and
guaze cloth
weaned at normal
weaning time
cropped
conditioned through
with unstruck sound

variation:

The introduction of light was not in itself disturbing, so long as other environmental factors remained stable.

variation:

always exploring
a degree of psychic
freedom from within
the perameters
of the certainties
the safeties of movement

2

What we don't say, inevitably
punctuated by what we do

infuriating
unrelenting semantics
shortening the rest periods
or dispensing with them:
an absence of all visual cues.
Waiting for the tranquility

denied, something else is here

3

Asleep. Once again or was it just once? If one eye is covered, the fast phase of interference turns towards the other eye. Turning. If both eyes open, wait for nystagmus to settle. Direction of jerks unrelated to directional light source.

It's difficult to speak in here. Not really alone and yet not really with anybody. An ambiguous silence.

4

As it advances and I fall into thinking of the situation one way or the other, it may well become easy to speak. Saying anything at all that comes to mind: the next thing I know, I haven't said anything. Say something about that then.

5

always comes to my lips
unbidden
to get out.
I have the thought
undeniable,
that this should stop.
A get out,
a struggle for
not much longer
not talking
straight
that's all.
Unable to...
everything in place
upon the distant shore.
Time ago
beneath the sun,
distinctions
passing through
as if altercating
the lines of things
gently
smearing the boundaries
with damping.
The ninth,
emphatic deletion.
Three sisters
on the way
to a field of dens.
The arc upon turning
of a friend.

6

variation:

An urgent need to survive the situation: in each instance of effort the artificial stress activates intense character defence mechanisms, pulling it further and sealing it in.

variation:

the notion here
 that the body
 is itself a mind
equally
 the inescapable
 physical bordering
of sentience:
 mind as manifest being
 possible to occlude
 and divide
into two components
 over there, the body
and over here
 at the teeth
 a scar
now heeled
and undertrod:
 a brick of skat

variation:

Or is it? Like this: In the matrix terrain, the inlock continues and is inseverable.

The sides are pressing in. When the signal is sounded, although I should easily unseal me, I will be unable to move. I know.

I am raining
I am raining inside
a rawfire, latitude dreaming me; arriving in lumps. Hanging from the lips of pipes. Spikes. Chained, pinioned; a cabinet fastened over exhaustion. Galvanised. The welcoming mania. In here. Ice-bound. A tether. Incarceration, leash, peg and tether. It's hot. Breathe then. It's hot...
movement trawls
ploughs skin
scar tissue
cranes, buildings
palpitations
the inclasp
contort, wreathe, intwine
the furore of
dead ends, driven
a vermicular
sliver
teeth
and
nail
and
and
sweat, heart slipping

phrenetic, latitude dreamed up by me. Written whilst falling. Hanging rough shod with rage. The energumen. Thrown out of gear. Berserk in it. Incite me. And I... incite me and I...
the earth is too heavy
sometimes the sea
always, diffusion
of the central node
of ferocity
interred in
hysteria
interior
turning
ratcheting the irritant
carbuncle, latitude dreamt out of me. Rolled up in blankets, sheets. Wrapped tight and then hosed down. A boiling stream. The cotton shrinks, constricting. Lungs sucked, the deeper nightfire hues. Straining. To squeeze out. To choke up. Mouthfuls, pages of it. Pulped. And trapped. The cornered hearts of spillages. Rickets cooling the hips. A helix chill...
the stabbing
at antrum
at tantrum
gnashing
a red rag
of thralldom:
explode then
– it's too tight to...
explode then
– torsion included...
explode
then the tendrill
concordia discours
any time close
to Saturnalia
with arms up

protecting the head
ribbons of wits
flitting the air
spatback
at the shredder
a surplus
pertusion, longitude dreamt up by me. A prison ship. (
lowerworld. A hole in earth. Knuckles bled out fro
thumping. A cabinet. Chained up to the grim lips of
juggernaut tyre. 'The sky is too heavy'. Is too, the sky...
and the soil is spat out
at the soil
concluding
a dirt-curtain
coruscation
glimpsed
and then sunk
into seven senses
each one
vacuums
the light behind and then

holds it out front
dazzling the foramina
a trapdoor
stirs
in its tunnel
throating
at meagre rays
a lantern of diogenes
– curl towards it –
chinks in the surdity
plunge an arm through
fingers groping
the distance
drills whirr up

through walls
a second arm
punched through
inscribing, scrawling
the blockade
drill whistles
scribbling the bone
before notching
the anchorite
a stump orator
pinioned, held fast
by swarms of brachial dust
the distance completed
with spray
a tendril signature
of curved moments
– it's raining
in here
I am raining

Litany

Earth is a ladder to clamber these faeces, a dead wall rising squarely, inclination irreal. The well-bottom sounded, eyes fixed at the firing stars to hook and pull out. Evulsioned onto the residue, a solution to drowning.

Saliva coeval with sky and earth, reborn through even the sharpest vinegar. Conflagration extinguished, bottle the phlogiston, nova of the first water. Head out to the hilly country to get this stuff barred.

Gas is interred, circular breathing holding the mass. The slightest variation in here will shatter the crop, the dial of suns melting and steaming the seal.

Fire of non-quantified numbering, the furnace itself, calcified through redemption. A room set aside, closed to the outside world. A stove is installed and regulated through suffocating the entrances. Escape patterns evaporate out of a ragged grease running the walls as compounds are indicated, excavating infernos. Equlibrate contagions that eat into cries.

North
is eternal in this white light
an ear-lobe as radar.
Frontal parietal amplitude waves
and sharp spikes of flame
occipital contouring

beneath
is a feeler, involuntary galvanism
shredding the omphalos encasing it

dexterity
is vivid and aglow
unavailable and cack-actioned

west
of the brachial paralysis
the hand should be raised above
the height of the shoulder
and pinned by the sleeve
slightly north.
External rotation at the elbow
supination leading down and away.
A stylus is grasped
and jabbed at equators.

Exuviating The Text

There is a modality within the endeavour of exuviating a text which conspires to maximise enunciation of the anatomy from which it is impelled. That this anatomy may be self or otherwise may be defused at its beginning by introducing a mediating figure...

The serpent:

As solus ipse extending
the fruit of knowledge
an image
of the fecund text
impregnated with pen and ink
snake and fruit

otherwise
the ouroboros
activating
ingestion of
the extinguished tail
snake and then loop

Both images, unsatisfactory... (en)gendered. A third: the serpent, subtle, self-begotten, doubled and twined as a caduceus, black and now white around a staff of winged Hermes. No, we must search again for serpentine trails of text. It always marches on its belly.

The problem that is taken to task in proposing to write the anatomy is the problem of anatomy itself as related through the crucibles and alembics of Alchemy. To attempt the transmutation of base alloys into gold seems a curious metaphor for the inevitability of failure but is in fact an act of decoy providing locomotion for a concealed interpolation of spirit into matter. The gold is for fools. Thus when considering the notion of transmuting anatomy into text, one should account the literal failure as of no consequence. What is of value is the variegated incidental yield issuing above its tegument.

One can speak then of a tendency towards substantiating the element through which the text propels. This is its first relation, first cause. There is a type of language that involves no arbitrary gesturing between physical utterance and its semantic impact. In this, a sign may be positioned in order to congeal its object through manifesting a measure of its qualities. This world is often lost though poetry exists to alchemise its traces.

Neither this or that word imparts more nor less of a tactility: it is in their conjunctions and juxtapositions, their clandestine affinities and repulsions that physical form is gained or lost. This conviction may result from living apart from the vehicular dimension of speech. In its place arrives discord, rhythm, repetition, abrupt shifts, accumulating, piling on of words producing a physical impact resonant of an irritant compulsion towards an authentic register confronting its anatomical intelligence.

What is written, striving to confirm the corporeality guiding its demarcation into being. Anchoring into the body, its blood, a type of faith in the fixity of what is real.

Engaging the undeniably corporeal status of the text rather than attempting to divert from or ignore it, a choice arises between the act of presenting or representing. Between counting and recounting. Consider the body as an item of populace, registered into an act of counting. Only later compelled to recount the events surrounding its evolution into an intersection for the cognisance of matter.

One may consider the quality of physical engagement evoked by a spagyric compilation in the conjunctions of signs, relationships between the rhythmic indices, reflexes triggered by the propositions that are attached to words... as being neither more nor less than an enunciation of anatomy, its armoury and liberty.

Writing the isomorph; a gyroscopic mapping of the presence guiding its inscription. The action of the book is compounded at an interstice between voice and autograph, thereby re-affixing the prototype estrangement between flesh and empyrean.

One arrives at an etymology of screams, anatomy of mind, which cannot hang fire to arbitrate with words. Within the scream, a voice is wired to involuntary convulsions from the bedrock of its impacted sensibilities. Emotion *is* the emission, in which there is no call to anatomise with words.

Consider once more, the serpent: a linguasomatic word is needed to define an action which fuses anatomy with earth; communicates the quiddity of death. An action which is precultural and could be used as analogue to the generation of text. This is from within, without. Pushing against skin, hefting, steamlifting the peeling integument, stripping: exuviating the text.

Patina

Cunctation of the adage, a wiper face: consult the next
page; it spits as you lift it

matriculation ticktacked, a swampum, some sump herein

octaves emitting a mould of breath, clung down as
forge-cack: a handle and

bevelled into entera

beginning at the kind of gleam that's always under the
block

its bridle, extrusioned as abutment

shoulderblades, dentures, other clausatives

a visceral fixture: do not give it your notice

No teeth! No other residency but in the pressurised fluvia

adjoining hot tongs, calefacient and loading

a peninsula, an architectural swivelling

cross-bred between expectorations, the found slot

hawking at the centrifuge

centripetal cusp

intransitive from having kindred in its groin

scratching and tracing iridescent synergies

this locus is nibbling a fritterment of cadence

Grounded into a cleanly pierced wound and naming it
with husks of grafted skin as portion to the soul:

the angle of the real is lowered to the vertex of the heart

cyphers running the cramped congruities

resilient, pulled around vibrato lips

slipping in the clasp of panic

an undertow of sludge and gasps

wormdrilling through microcircuitries of tears

and milk

the bible-shades of radared rot

its prismal larva

into the sucking of mandible sparoid carn

emerging the crucifer spack of its world

shaken, driven to sepsis, marmoreal in amplitude

the craw-lode stitched back between fixed points

between the power and of course its fury

where the waters are twining the mastoid branches

with the carapace scrambling the distance above us

A word that speaks from its quagmired ditch: ACELDAMA

fields of blood

the umbilical spit of blazing streams

creamed and warm, a fossilised infinite vehicle of dreams

captured in tegument

skin constraining the leaping crimson

under the bludgeoning tilt of the skies

the needlework of scriveners dipping within

filtering out of its milk and semen

spit

drawn off, choked and strangling

the wipe of it smearing multiple chins

cut

unleashed into the breath

into a skein of blood

thickening its plasmic surface

and the quill is loading the fortified pneuma

and the ink is mixed at the fount of the neck

Malo

Body drumming

bitten between teeth

Malo hears voices

– *Malo is voice but the voices are ears...*

resonates to all other organs

the tonal inlays

emanation
sonic residue
matrices

...found oneself in the dark, and if not exactly...

an abrupt entry into the scars of sound

came to listen to the atmospheric shifts

...listen to atmosphere, it shifts...

Malo is multilunged

cavernous, panoptic

fathoming the dome of stars

and layering its chimes

avascular

mute

obliviating

At the end of the book are its voices. These are the shrapnel, slid into the spine, which activate its rages. Without devising a constellar art, they are what we have come to this for. No voice, no book. Your voice almost imperceptibly repeating this. I hear it now. Here. 'Blooded under a conspiracy of residue'. You read it and say it. Without movement, and still it clatters my pages.

I have come to this: it is indecent to speak of one's functioning in I. The membrum virile, paraphiliac, flashing the solus ipse. The voice resists: initiation compounds us elsewhere. And vacuums out of the mess: '...this to come have I.'

Forthwith Malo.

Malo: male-o, baddo. The heart of Malo. Malodorous, marl. And also, malleus: the hammer. Halo. The male-o. As well, imperfect. Defective.

Malo is taking part in a book. In order to do so, he endeavours at re-membering the anatomy and physiology of speech as if, in some way, he could enchant those for whom the book waits. Soon, it is apparent that each organ concerned with speech production is so only secondarily to some other more urgent function – respiration, swallowing, lubricance. Eating and chewing food. Malo decides to place these first, too. Now, when struggling at the console of the switchboard he contrived (to mediate the surges and absences within the book), all he hears at first is the heaving at the diaphragm, swilling sluices, moans and bolts.

The solution is direct. Malo is extirpating the vocal tract with knives. In sleep: the stealth of his hand as it slides through his mouth, down, past the snarlings of his larynx to the cavernous holes of the burning thorax. The blade, tiny and swift betwixt efferent fingers, flickers at the neural raiment. Malo, an ouroboros circling in the night. At work, filleting the noisome kit.

And in the morning, severed from its mortal casing, the bladderlung hangs loose inside, punctured and sucked of its breath. When the sun draws its legion, it is to spit itself, inverted into the air with a last momentous spasm.

The voice is to be rebuilt. To voice: a verb. To utter somehow in words. Now, everything moves in its signal box, bristling with activity. The walls, curious with lettering, fluctuate precisely to the workings of its heart. Without oral features, parts of the book arrive. Malo becomes hand signals. Leg kicks. A rib begins to knit itself illegibly, around adjacent ribs. We are wiring in. Drunk with intrusions. Squalls of supersaturating sonic, a cacklebabble shunting through its haywire sermoning, scouring for its screed. This is the lodestar. Its holythroat. Convening at the neck with host imbibers. Randomly. A Holythroat Symposium.

Addendum

The central design
in conducting 'A Holythroat Symposium'
was to fortify the conjunction
between
a sense of identity
evolving from out of the physical situation
or 'hors de combat'
of deafness
and the ongoing exertion
and problem
of engendering texts.
That is,
to oscillate between
what has become congested
into a state of anatomy
and the mechanical synopsis of its trace
thereby
diminishing the distance
of its seesawing
to this end.

The primary source of identification
the body

as residue
conducting fulgurative interrogations
of the phonic
in and around language
yet to one side of its drag.

Or: I am nervous about life
the irrigation of its dreaming
cataclinal
yet never ceasing
with the pooling of itself
amounting to these cries:
these cries which are also
invaginations
at the tip of a stiletto.

First, the title.
I wanted to suggest
the sancticity of vocalisation
as anatomical process
within an environment
that is usually normalising it
into an activity which is granted.
By proposing a 'holiness'
to speech
the work may begin to imitate
an archaic convention
of ascribing anatomical residence
for god
as being inside the voice:
a voice which is not only
the voice of its speech.

The throat
in its turn
suggests a physiognomy
a concrete metonymic specification
– the block on which this threnody
is measured off –
'throttled out of its thrombotic thoroughfare'

Symposium:
initially
a meeting of people
for the purpose of inebriation
– a hidden flaw
subsiding liabilities
in upholding myths
(talking activities) –
around forms
whilst contemplating an ideological status
for a specific one:
the body of work as it
pulls at its ballast.

The writing then, addresses issues
which, overlapping,
are stated repeatedly
– failing in a sense, its oto-reception –
repeatedly
from out of separate soundsource or contexts:
a holythroat symposium.